MR. FUSSY

by Roger Hargreaves

Mr Fussy was fussy about everything.

Absolutely everything had to be neat and tidy and in its proper place.

Mr Fussy spent all day and every day rearranging his furniture, and making sure the flowers grew in a straight line in his garden, and trying to find specks of dust where there couldn't possibly be specks of dust because he spent all his time making sure there weren't any specks of dust.

One fine morning, Mr Fussy was having breakfast.

He was very fussy about what he ate.

He opened the marmalade pot.

"Ugh!" he exclaimed. "It's got bits in it!"

And he spent the rest of the morning separating the bits from the marmalade. Or, if you prefer, the marmalade from the bits.

"Fussy old fusspot" people used to call him.

Then Mr Fussy went out into his garden.

And spent the rest of the day straightening out all the blades of grass on his lawn!

Fussy old fusspot!

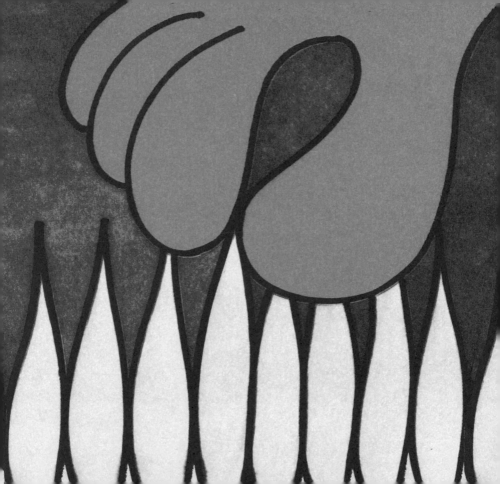

That evening Mr Fussy was in his kitchen (ironing his shoelaces) when he heard a crash outside.

"What's to do?" he murmured to himself, and hurried outside to investigate.

There, with a broken garden gate in one hand, an old battered suitcase in the other, and a sheepish grin on his face, stood an untidy person.

Mr Clumsy!

"Whoops!" he said, holding up the garden gate. "It came off in my hand!"

"Who," spluttered Mr Fussy, looking in horror at his garden gate, "are you?"

"I'm Mr Clumsy," replied the untidy person grinning, and he stepped forward to shake Mr Fussy's hand, but tripped over and fell on the lawn.

"My grass," cried Mr Fussy. "My straight grass. You've bent it!"

And he got down on his hands and knees, and started straightening the grass.

"But who are you?" he asked over his shoulder. "And why are you here?"

"I'm your cousin," replied Mr Clumsy. "Your long lost cousin from Australia. I've come to visit."

"Aren't you pleased to see me?" continued Mr Clumsy cheerfully, knocking over a flower or two as he got up, and picked up his suitcase, knocking over another flower or two, or three.

Mr Fussy, quite obviously, wasn't pleased to see him.

"You'd better come in," he muttered.

"I say," remarked Mr Clumsy, looking through the front door of Mr Fussy's house, "I say, what a neat little place you've got here!"

And he stepped inside, and tripped over his shoelaces (he often does), and knocked over a chair, and dropped his suitcase, and fell in an untidy heap on the floor.

"Whoops," he said.

Mr Fussy shut his eyes, and heaved a sigh, and groaned silently to himself.

Later that evening, after Mr Fussy had cooked them a meal, and after Mr Clumsy had helped with the washing up (two broken plates), they sat down to talk.

Mr Fussy sat, as he always did, in a neat and tidy fashion.

Mr Clumsy sat, as he always did, in a not so neat and tidy fashion.

"How long are you staying?" asked Mr Fussy.

"Oh, I don't know," grinned Mr Clumsy. "A few days. A week. A year. I haven't decided."

When he awoke in the morning, Mr Fussy jumped out of bed and went into his bathroom.

"Oh no," he gasped. "Oh no!"

Oh yes!

Mr Clumsy had been there before him.

The towels lay in a heap on the floor.

The bath was full of water.

There were pools of water all over the bathroom floor, and, half a tube of toothpaste!

What a mess!

Mr Fussy made it all neat and tidy as quickly as he could.

Then Mr Fussy hurried downstairs.

"Morning," said his cousin cheerfully. "I've cooked you breakfast. Sit down!"

There was an awful mess everywhere.

"There we are," said Mr Clumsy, carrying a plate of fried eggs (broken fried eggs) towards the table. "Breakfast!"

And then he tripped over those shoelaces of his, and then the eggs flew through the air, and then they landed all over Mr Fussy.

Sticky, greasy, yellow, fried eggs!

"Whoops," said Mr Clumsy.

After a week, Mr Fussy's house didn't look like Mr Fussy's house any more at all.

But, after two weeks, Mr Clumsy decided to move on.

"Thank you for having me," he said to Mr Fussy.

"It was very nice to see you," replied Mr Fussy politely.

But what he was thinking was, "It's very nice to see you going."

"Cheerio," said Mr Clumsy, and off he went with his battered old suitcase.

"Goodbye," called Mr Fussy, really meaning, "Good riddance!"

Then Mr Fussy fussed around his house as he'd never fussed before.

Fussy old fusspot!

Polishing, and mending, and repairing, and straightening, and sorting out, and cleaning, and putting everything back exactly as it had been before Mr Clumsy had come to stay.

He even dusted the flowers in the garden!

That evening Mr Fussy was in his kitchen (polishing an egg) when he heard a crash outside.

"Oh no," he groaned. "Not Mr Clumsy back again. It can't be! It mustn't be! It isn't!"

And it wasn't!

It was somebody else.

Somebody who had just walked straight through Mr Fussy's garden gate.

Somebody who can't help having little accidents.

Somebody you may have met before.

"Hello," smiled Mr Bump.

"I've come to visit!"

3 Great Offers for MR. MEN Fans!

MR. MEN TOKEN

1 New Mr. Men or Little Miss Library Bus Presentation Cases

A brand new stronger, roomier school bus library box, with sturdy carrying handle and stay-closed fasteners.
The full colour, wipe-clean boxes make a great home for your full collection.
They're just £5.99 inc P&P and free bookmark!

☐ MR. MEN ☐ LITTLE MISS (please tick and order overleaf)

2 Door Hangers and Posters

PLEASE STICK YOUR 50P COIN HERE

In every Mr. Men and Little Miss book like this one, you will find a special token. Collect 6 tokens and we will send you a brilliant Mr. Men or Little Miss poster and a Mr. Men or Little Miss double sided full colour bedroom door hanger of your choice. Simply tick your choice in the list and tape a 50p coin for your two items to this page.

Door Hangers (please tick)
☐ Mr. Nosey & Mr. Muddle
☐ Mr. Slow & Mr. Busy
☐ Mr. Messy & Mr. Quiet
☐ Mr. Perfect & Mr. Forgetful
☐ Little Miss Fun & Little Miss Late
☐ Little Miss Helpful & Little Miss Tidy
☐ Little Miss Busy & Little Miss Brainy
☐ Little Miss Star & Little Miss Fun

Posters (please tick)
☐ MR. MEN
☐ LITTLE MISS

3 Sixteen Beautiful Fridge Magnets – any 2 for £2.00! inc.P&P

They're very special collector's items!
Simply tick your first and second* choices from the list below
of any 2 characters!

1st Choice
- ☐ Mr. Happy
- ☐ Mr. Lazy
- ☐ Mr. Topsy-Turvy
- ☐ Mr. Bounce
- ☐ Mr. Bump
- ☐ Mr. Small
- ☐ Mr. Snow
- ☐ Mr. Wrong

- ☐ Mr. Daydream
- ☐ Mr. Tickle
- ☐ Mr. Greedy
- ☐ Mr. Funny
- ☐ Little Miss Giggles
- ☐ Little Miss Splendid
- ☐ Little Miss Naughty
- ☐ Little Miss Sunshine

2nd Choice
- ☐ Mr. Happy
- ☐ Mr. Lazy
- ☐ Mr. Topsy-Turvy
- ☐ Mr. Bounce
- ☐ Mr. Bump
- ☐ Mr. Small
- ☐ Mr. Snow
- ☐ Mr. Wrong

- ☐ Mr. Daydream
- ☐ Mr. Tickle
- ☐ Mr. Greedy
- ☐ Mr. Funny
- ☐ Little Miss Giggles
- ☐ Little Miss Splendid
- ☐ Little Miss Naughty
- ☐ Little Miss Sunshine

*Only in case your first choice is out of stock.

TO BE COMPLETED BY AN ADULT

To apply for any of these great offers, ask an adult to complete the coupon below and send it with the appropriate payment and tokens, if needed, to MR. MEN OFFERS, PO BOX 7, MANCHESTER M19 2HD

☐ Please send _____ Mr. Men Library case(s) and/or _____ Little Miss Library case(s) at £5.99 each inc P&P

☐ Please send a poster and door hanger as selected overleaf. I enclose six tokens plus a 50p coin for P&P

☐ Please send me _____ pair(s) of Mr. Men/Little Miss fridge magnets, as selected above at £2.00 inc P&P

Fan's Name _____

Address _____

_____ **Postcode** _____

Date of Birth _____

Name of Parent/Guardian _____

Total amount enclosed £ _____

☐ **I enclose a cheque/postal order payable to Egmont Books Limited**

☐ **Please charge my MasterCard/Visa/Amex/Switch or Delta account** (delete as appropriate)

Card Number

Expiry date ___/___   **Signature** _____

MR.MEN   LITTLE MISS
Mr. Men and Little Miss™ & ©Mrs. Roger Hargreaves

CUT ALONG DOTTED LINE AND RETURN THIS WHOLE PAGE